CHARACTER COUNTS!®

A Roar of Respect

By Jenne Simon

Illustrated by Kasia Nowowiejska

SCHOLASTIC INC.

ISBN 978-1-338-03341-0

10 9 8 7 6 5 4 3 2 1   16 17 18 19 20

Printed in the U.S.A.   40
First printing, September 2016
Designed by Angela Jun

Mr. Pillar had big news to share with his class.

"We are putting on a play," said Mr. Pillar. The class got excited.

They could not wait to hear the audience cheer for their show.

"But we have a lot to do to get ready," said the teacher.

Everyone agreed that Lang the Lion would be the perfect director.
His friends really needed his help.

They were all so excited to show off their talents that they got a little carried away!

Kiara and Emilio both loved the spotlight, so they would be the actors. Handy Gus would build the set.

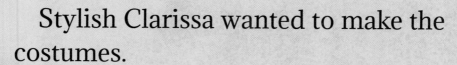

Stylish Clarissa wanted to make the costumes.

Brooke knew how to play the piano and offered to be in charge of music.

"Lang, can you please tell Emilio that the princess is the main character?" cried Kiara. "I should have more lines!"

"Tell her the wizard is way more important," Emilio argued.

"We should cut both of your lines to make room for an extra song," said Brooke.

Lang tried to calm everyone down.
"There is no need to fight," he said.
"I'm here to help."

Lang went to check on Gus.
The castle set he had built was amazing.

But the stage was so crowded. There was barely room for the actors!

Clarissa had been busy.
She had made colorful costumes that shined in the light.

But the outfits were so over-the-top, it was hard for the actors to walk and talk in them!

Soon the whole class was arguing. Everyone wanted to be in the spotlight, and they were not doing a good job of sharing it.

The play was going to be a disaster!
Lang knew he had to do something.

Lang gathered his classmates.
"We need to work together to make
this play a success," he said.

"Putting on a play is a team effort,"
he said. "None of us can do it alone.
We need to respect one another to be a
good team!"

Everyone nodded.

Lang was right — they had to help one another.

The show must go on!

Soon it was showtime.
And what a show it was!

When the play
was over, the audience
cheered.

The loudest applause was for Lang!

The crowd quieted down as Mr. Pillar took the stage.

"One of my students deserves special thanks," said Mr. Pillar.

He placed a shiny gold medal around Lang's neck.

"This is for showing us all the true meaning of respect," said Mr. Pillar. "Bravo!"